GETTING
HOME

ATTACK ON EARTH

GETTING HOME

STEPHANIE PERRY MOORE

darbycreek

MINNEAPOLIS

30988 1769

R

Darby Creek
A division of Lerner Publishing Group, Inc.
241 First Avenue North
Minneapolis, MN 55401 USA

For reading levels and more information, look up this title at www.lernerbooks.com.

The images in this book are used with the permission of: Ollyy/Shutterstock.com; briddy_/iStock/Getty Images; ilobs/iStock/Getty Images; 4khz/DigitalVision Vectors/ Getty Images.

Main body text set in Janson Text LT Std 12/17.5.
Typeface provided by Adobe Systems.

Library of Congress Cataloging-in-Publication Data

Names: Moore, Stephanie Perry, author.
Title: Getting home / Stephanie Perry Moore.
Description: Minneapolis : Darby Creek, [2018] | Series: Attack on Earth | Summary: High school senior Bailey Clarke and her younger brother, Blake, must trust strangers to help them reach their father's home when an alien invasion causes their bus to break down.
Identifiers: LCCN 2017049272 (print) | LCCN 2017060634 (ebook) | ISBN 9781541525856 (eb pdf) | ISBN 9781541525757 (lb : alk. paper) | ISBN 9781541526280 (pb : alk. paper)
Subjects: | CYAC: Survival—Fiction. | Interpersonal relations—Fiction. | Brothers and sisters—Fiction. | African Americans—Fiction. | Extraterrestrial beings—Fiction. | Science fiction.
Classification: LCC PZ7.M788125 (ebook) | LCC PZ7.M788125 Gg 2018 (print) | DDC [Fic]—dc23

LC record available at https://lccn.loc.gov/2017049272

Manufactured in the United States of America
1-44559-35490-2/12/2018

TO MY LITTLE BROTHER, FRANKLIN DENNIS
PERRY JR. OH, THE ADVENTURES WE TOOK
GROWING UP. THANKFUL WE ALWAYS HAD
EACH OTHER'S BACKS. MAY EVERY READER
KNOW HOME IS IN THE HEART AS LONG AS YOU
TAKE CARE OF THOSE YOU LOVE.

ON THE MORNING OF FRIDAY, OCTOBER 2, rings of light were seen coming down from the sky in several locations across the planet. By mid-morning, large spacecraft were visible through the clouds, hovering over major cities. The US government, along with others, attempted to make contact, without success.

At 9:48 that morning, the alien ships released an electromagnetic pulse, or EMP, around the world, disabling all electronics—including many vehicles and machines. All forms of communication technology were useless.

Now people could only wait and see what would happen with the "Visitors" next . . .

CHAPTER 1

We were on a bus ride from Atlanta, Georgia, to Montgomery, Alabama, when the blast came. The trip had started badly—with Momma giving me a lecture about taking care of my younger brother, Blake, while we visited our dad—and it hadn't gotten better from there. For the past hour, the guy in front of us had been talking loudly on his phone about a college visit that had gone wrong and had refused to move his seatback up when Blake had asked him to. The white couple sitting across the aisle were bickering about something. Everyone else on the bus seemed to be gossiping about the alien spaceships that had appeared this morning.

I'd been trying not to look at my phone. I knew my inbox would be full of texts from Momma back in Atlanta or from Dad in Montgomery. And my newsfeed would be clogged with coverage of the so-called Visitors. I couldn't believe people thought it was real.

After the bus had made its first stop on the route, we'd been traveling back to the interstate highway when we suddenly heard a strange buzzing sound. The tires skidded and screeched as the driver tried to keep control of the bus. It began to turn and the front half shot off the pavement and into a ditch next to the road. Everyone began screaming as they slammed forward into the seatbacks.

My phone fell out of my hand as my head jerked into the seat in front of me. "You okay?" I asked Blake. I reached down to grab my phone from the floor. A vehicle must have been coming down the road behind us—it rammed into the side of the bus toward the back.

Then another vehicle slammed into the bus. I tumbled into the aisle, but before I could get too far, the guy sitting in front of us grabbed my shoulders to steady me.

My ears were ringing and my eyes had trouble focusing. I could hardly hear anything over everyone's panicked screams. "Thanks," I mumbled to the guy. He helped me back to my seat. In the back of my mind I registered that this was the same jerk who wouldn't move up his seatback when my brother asked. Instead he'd spent the entire bus ride yelling defensively into his phone about "not my fault" and "someone must've planted those steroids on me."

"Bailey!" my brother called out to me. He stared at me with wide eyes.

"What's wrong?" I asked.

Now that I had enough time to look, I could see that Blake's right foot was hanging inward at an awkward angle that made my stomach flip. He pulled up the leg of his jeans with shaky hands and revealed a rapidly swelling ankle. "It slammed into the wall when we crashed," he explained.

Fifty percent of me wanted to holler, but the other fifty percent took over, keeping me calm. I moved Blake's leg so it could rest on my seat. Then I grabbed my phone to search for how to take care of an injury like this, only to realize my phone had died. The calm started to slip away.

"Somebody help me!" I spun around in a circle, looking for anyone to help us. "Please! My brother is hurt."

"What's wrong?" the guy from the seat in front of us asked. He peered around the seat and his eyes widened when he saw Blake's foot.

He took a deep breath then gave Blake a quick smile. "Let's take a look at that."

I stepped aside in surprise. The guy couldn't have been much older than me— seventeen or eighteen, I would guess. But I could barely think, and I didn't know if my fingers would work even if I wanted them to, so I was ready to let just about anyone help at this point.

"Doesn't look too bad. Might just be a sprain," he said. Then he looked around at the bags we had tucked beneath the seats. Most of it had shifted, so my backpack was shoved too far under another seat to reach it. He pulled his belt loose from around his pants. "Does anyone have anything that can be used as a brace?" he asked loudly.

"I have a pair of knitting needles," the woman sitting across the aisle from us said. "Would that work?"

"Better than nothing," the guy said.

She pulled the knitting needles from her bag and quickly handed them over. He looked at the man sitting next to her. "Can I use your belt too, sir? And your sweater, ma'am?"

Armed with a yellow sweater, two belts, and a pair of knitting needles, the guy turned back to my brother. "What's your name?" he asked, rolling up the jeans so they were neatly cuffed just below Blake's knee.

"Blake."

"Nice to meet you, Blake. I'm Colby. This might hurt a little, but you're gonna be okay." Blake nodded bravely.

Colby wrapped the sweater around Blake's foot and ankle, tugging the sleeves into a tight knot. Then he lined up the needles on either side of Blake's leg and secured them using both belts.

"Well, that should keep it stabilized for now," he said. "Till we can find something better."

"Thank you so much," I said as he stood. I moved to sit next to Blake. "How did you know how to do that?"

Colby shrugged. "I play football—you get pretty used to setting injuries."

Blake eyed the letterman jacket Colby was wearing. "Hey, you're Colby Grant! You're one of the best safeties in the state."

I had no idea who that was, but Blake followed high school and college football religiously. I was just happy to see that he didn't seem to be in too much pain.

"What's going on out there?" the man across the aisle asked. His wife had pressed her head against the window, trying to get a look at the road ahead of us. Bailey and I tried to see out our window too.

There weren't many other vehicles on the road. But with damaged cars smashed into the front and back of our bus, there was no way it would be able to get off the street.

Nervous voices rose inside the bus, and the bus driver stood up to face us. "Okay, everyone, just calm down!" he shouted.

"Where are we?" someone in the front asked.

It was impossible to tell. We were on an empty country road, with nothing but trees and fields on either side of us. There weren't even signs along the street giving mile markers. I tried to remember how long we'd been on the road. It was about a four-hour trip from Atlanta to Montgomery, and it had been nearly two hours since we said good-bye to Momma and climbed aboard the bus. That first bus station we'd stopped at had looked like it was in the middle of nowhere. I had no idea where the nearest town was.

"I think my phone died when I dropped it," I said, turning to Blake. "Can you check where we are?"

Blake held up his phone and looked at it in surprise. He showed me the screen—also black. "I was just playing a game on it before we crashed. That's weird."

I turned to the couple sitting across from us. "Um, excuse me, can either of you check where we are?"

They both pulled out their cell phones and looked at them in surprise. "My battery must have died," the woman said. She started digging through her bag. "My charger is in here somewhere."

"Is anyone's phone working?" someone called out then. Everyone seemed to be checking their phones, and none of them seemed to work.

"The radio is dead too," the bus driver said. "I can't get in touch with the station."

People began to panic again. The rising voices made my head spin again. Blake started to shift, but he hissed and quickly reached for his leg, rubbing at it tenderly just above the makeshift ankle brace. "It really hurts," he said.

"Just sit back. You're gonna be okay," I told him, trying to keep calm. He was only thirteen. He was always fighting with Momma about how he was old enough to do things on his own, but I could see from the look on his face that, deep down, he was freaking out.

"All right, all right," the bus driver said, raising his hands. He lifted the cap off his head and wiped the sweat away from his face. Then he let out a long breath of air, glancing back at the bus's dead dashboard.

Everyone had quieted, waiting as if he'd be able to give us some sort of answer.

He looked out the windows, then back at us. "For starters, let's all get off the bus. Some fresh air might do us all good."

Having something—anything—to do seemed to make people feel better already. This was familiar. We could all handle collecting our luggage and getting off the bus. Everyone immediately jumped into action, gathering as many of their belongings as they could and filing out of the bus.

I had managed to yank my backpack from under the seat and find Blake's. But Blake was already taller than me—and heavier—so I could barely do more than help him stand up.

Seeing me struggle, Colby stepped in and let Blake wrap an arm around his shoulder. The couple next to us offered to help carry our things as we made our way off the bus.

The five of us picked a spot in the grass. The trees were farther away than Blake seemed ready to walk, and the fall morning sun was hot for this time of year, but at least we were outside and no longer breathing in the stale air of the bus.

We checked Blake's ankle. It would probably need to be x-rayed and looked at by a doctor, but this setup was better than nothing. "Thanks for all your help," I said to the others.

"I'm Allison," the woman introduced herself. "This is my husband John." She looked at Blake and me. "Are you two traveling alone?"

"Yeah, we're supposed to spend the fall break with our dad in Montgomery." I left it at that. No point in telling this stranger that we wouldn't have to make this trip if our dad hadn't abandoned us for a cushy job in another state. Momma kept telling me I was being dramatic about it. In my opinion, I was just keeping it real.

"How are we gonna get in touch with Dad?" Blake asked me. "He'll be worried when he doesn't hear from us."

"I wouldn't worry about that right now," I told him, thinking of all the times in the past year that our father had not made us a priority.

After about a half hour of sitting around, we noticed some people were beginning to walk down the long stretch of highway. With my brother's ankle swollen and darkness just a few hours away, walking was the last thing I wanted to do. But doing what I wanted wasn't a choice. We were stuck here, and walking the other half of the way to get to my dad seemed to be the smartest option.

"Do you have some ice in your pack?" Colby asked me.

"Yeah, some." Momma had packed us each a lunch for the bus ride. I quickly dug into the insulated lunch bag to grab a handful of ice cubes.

"Wrap some in this," he said as he handed me a towel with the Hillview University logo on it. "We've gotta leave. We need him strong."

"Nice towel," I remarked. Hillview was one of the top schools in northern Georgia. It was well known for its impressive athletic programs. "Do you go there?"

His face fell. "Nah. I was just there on a recruiting visit, but . . ."

I remembered the snippets of his phone conversation that I'd overheard—something about "not my fault" and steroids being planted. "Didn't go so well?"

"Yeah. I'd rather not get into it." He looked away.

While Colby and I talked, the adults had been arguing about what we should do. I longed for my parents so they could tell us the answer. I also wished my cell was working so I could call them and let them know we were okay. But was that a true statement? Was being stranded in the middle of nowhere with an injured brother really okay?

As I finished wrapping the ice around Blake's ankle, a foul odor hit my nose—gasoline.

"It's a leak," John said. "We've gotta get away from this bus now."

Some people still seemed reluctant to leave. Colby looked down at where I was kneeling and said, "I don't know what anyone else is doing, but gather your stuff. We're getting out of here."

He said it like we were a team. I didn't know him. However, I'd seen enough disaster movies to know that there was strength in numbers. I'd rather stick with this guy than be alone with my brother.

"Do you think it was them?" a man standing near us asked the man he was traveling with. "The Visitors?"

"Has to be," the other man said. "How else would all of our phones die at the same time? And the bus crash?" He gestured to the road where there was a buildup of crashed or stopped cars. "All the other cars are dead too. You think that's a coincidence?"

I couldn't hear the rest of their conversation as they made their way toward the road with their suitcase. My stomach dropped—I hadn't even thought about the Visitors.

The idea of venturing off into the unknown was scary enough on its own. I had no idea where we would go, which direction we needed to take. We had hardly any food on us, and we had nothing with us to provide shelter.

But thinking about the aliens—those so-called Visitors—made my heart speed up. What would they do next? Were they going to show themselves—attack us directly?

Don't think about that now, I told myself. I couldn't worry. As my mom had always told us, I needed to take care of the things I could control and not worry about the things I couldn't.

So, step one: we knew we had to start walking if we had any hope of finding our dad. After grabbing my things, I looked over at Blake. His backpack was on his back. Even with his injured foot, he was tough and ready to jet.

Before we could get moving, though, we faced another dilemma. As trivial as it seemed, we had to decide if we were going to take our luggage. The extra clothes, toiletries, and whatever else we had in our bags could help us survive, but the weight could slow us down.

"What do you wanna do, sis?" Blake asked me.

As I turned to respond to him, I was surprised to notice several of the others were watching me, listening to what I was about to say. Apparently everyone—even the adults—needed someone to tell them what to do at this point. "I think we should take our bags, and if they get too heavy or slow us down, we can always dump them later," I said. My brother nodded. I noticed that most everyone else did what Blake and I had agreed on.

I realized that until we were back with our parents, if I could just stay calm and think quick on my feet, we might actually be able to get through this okay.

Allison walked over to me. "Hey, are you guys still planning to go on to Montgomery?"

I looked over at Blake and nodded. "I think so."

"John and I talked it over—we were supposed to catch another bus in Montgomery before heading on, so we'd have to pass through there anyway to get home." She gave a nervous smile. "I know you don't know us, but we'd be happy to make sure you get there safe."

"I'd like that," I said, feeling myself tear up. The events of the day seemed to come crashing down on me all at once. I felt exhausted from all the arguing with Momma, worrying over Blake, and now trying to figure out what was happening. I was only seventeen—I had no idea what I was doing, but I knew Blake was looking to me for what we needed to do. Having someone else reach out and offer to look out for us, to take some of the burden off my shoulders, helped.

As Allison went back to her husband to grab their things, I took a shaky breath to calm myself. Colby was walking toward me, and I didn't want him to see me crying like this.

"Hey. We're gonna walk together, right?" he asked.

"Allison and John just invited us to walk with them too," I said, gesturing over to them. "If you're cool with that, you can come with us if you want." I felt my cheeks heat up, not sure why I was even asking him.

Colby shrugged. "Seems like we work well together. Yeah, I'll roll. Besides," he grinned at me, "if they try anything crazy, I got your back."

That surprised me. Earlier on the bus, he'd seemed like such a cocky jerk. But he'd been kind to me and Blake since the bus had crashed. I couldn't figure him out. It was nice to know yet another person was looking out for me, but I also knew I had my own back.

CHAPTER 2

It took us two hours to walk two miles. Everyone was exhausted—especially Blake. Our luggage wasn't easy to carry along the gravely roads, but we were still reluctant to leave it behind.

After a while, Colby and I ended up walking next to each other. He didn't say anything, but by then most of us were too tired to talk. I couldn't help myself from peeking over at him, though. I'd never thought much about boys before. And though I'd first figured he was just like all the other cocky athletes in my school, there was something different about Colby. I just couldn't quite figure out what it was yet.

I could feel Colby watching me. I glanced over at him.

"You look worried," he said quietly. "Don't be scared. Everything's going to be okay."

"How do you know?" I asked.

"I just do," he said, giving me another confident grin. It should have annoyed me, but instead I found myself smiling back at him.

After a few more minutes of walking, we came across a gas station. None of the lights were on, but John walked in to check it out.

We stayed hidden by a row of trees while we waited. Allison looked tense, chewing on her thumbnail as she stared at the door waiting for John.

"I'm sure he'll be fine," I said to her, placing my hand on her arm. "Everything will be just fine."

She smiled nervously but never kept her gaze off that door.

A few minutes later, John came back outside and waved us toward him. "Oh, thank goodness," Allison breathed.

"See?" I said, grinning at her. This time she gave me a wide smile in return.

"Yes!" my brother cheered. "I'm hungry." He trotted up to the door, not bothering to wait for the rest of us. *Of course now his ankle seems better,* I thought to myself. We laughed as we followed him.

"Thanks for all the help, Blake!" I teased, dragging our bags with me.

He stopped and turned to face me with a sheepish look on his face.

"Come on in, Master Blake," John said with a laugh. I shook my head at Blake, but I couldn't hold back my grin—I was too relieved at the thought that we'd found somewhere safe to stay the night. Blake realized he wasn't actually in trouble and sped into the building. The rest of us filed in after him.

"Everyone," John continued, "this is Stockey—he owns this place. He said we can help ourselves to anything in here."

A short man with a round belly and a bushy white mustache stood by the register. "Definitely get you some ice cream," Stockey told us, winking at Blake. "Because without the electricity, I'm gonna lose everything anyway."

Blake headed straight toward the freezer section, grabbing a bag of chips along the way, and I laughed. While our parents were probably worried sick and definitely wouldn't want us eating all this junk food, they'd be happy to know we were at least safe. I could only hope they were safe too.

Suddenly the shattering of glass startled us. Two men with masks rushed into the store.

"Everybody on the floor, now!" one of them shouted. He turned to Stockey, who was still standing behind the register. "We need money."

"I can't open the register. It's electronic," Stockey replied.

"Well, you'd better find a way to open it or someone is gonna get it," the other robber said, moving toward Blake.

Blake, who was still standing off to the side by the freezer section doors, went wide-eyed. He dropped the carton of ice cream in his hand and didn't seem to be able to move.

"Stay away from him!" I shouted, cutting through an aisle to get in front of Blake. I didn't care what happened to me. But if anyone was going to survive all this, it was going to be my brother.

CHAPTER 3

Since Blake and I were little, we'd had a way of communicating with each other without speaking. We'd goof off, silently working together to pull jokes on our parents. If one of us was running around the house while our parents chased them, the other one would sneak a snack out of the kitchen. Guess we had some sort of unspoken code, and it still worked even when we were older.

When I ran down the food aisle, the robber got startled. He didn't seem to know if he should look at me or at Blake. While I kept him distracted, Blake shoved him from behind. The robber stumbled forward, and I stuck my foot out to trip him. He rolled into the middle of the store, landing on his hands and knees.

Meanwhile, Colby had charged toward the first robber. He put his football skills to use and tackled the guy. They rolled, swinging their fists, but eventually Colby got him pinned.

"Are you all right?" Allison asked me. I nodded, panting to catch my breath. My hands were shaking from the adrenaline rush.

For a moment, we all just stood there while the two of them sat on the tiled floor in the middle of us. We had no idea what to do next.

"What do you want to do with them now?" John asked Stockey. "It's not like we can contact the police at the moment."

"I have rope," Stockey said. "We could tie them up."

"But you don't understand," the first robber insisted. "We didn't even have any weapons. We weren't really going to hurt anybody. We were just hungry and freaking out about the Visitors and . . . we didn't know what else to do."

John sighed. "That doesn't mean you can just come in and rob someone."

The other robber's face scrunched up like he was about to cry. "We just panicked. Everything's so messed up out there—we live a few miles away and everyone's already looted the stores. We barely got more than a few bottles of water and cans of soup."

Colby caught my eyes as if he was wondering what I was thinking. I didn't know what to think. What these guys tried to do was wrong, but I could understand how scared they felt.

I turned to Stockey. "What if we just let them go?" Everyone looked at me in surprise. I glared down at the guys sitting on the floor. "You leave now and never come back here, and don't try this nonsense with any other business."

They both nodded hastily. "Yeah. Of course," one said.

"Absolutely," the other added.

Everyone looked at Stockey to see what he thought—it was his store after all. He sighed and rubbed his hand over his face.

"Okay," he said. He waved a hand at them and barked, "Get out of here. Now! If I ever see either of you near here again . . ."

"You won't," the first one assured us. They stood up quickly and raced out of the store without looking back.

Colby walked to the door to watch that they didn't stop running. He turned the lock on the door with a heavy *thunk*.

We all let out shaky breaths. Stockey wandered into the back office, muttering to himself about needing something to take the edge off after all that. I leaned against a shelf as I fought to calm myself down. The thought of Blake getting hurt by someone had left me rattled.

Colby and John moved Blake to sit down so they could take a look at his ankle and make sure it was still set properly. I watched from a distance, not wanting my panicked feelings to stir up Blake even more.

Allison came over to me. "Earlier, I told you that I wanted you to come with me and John so we could make sure you all were safe.

But you were amazing back there. I'm actually glad we're with you so *we* can stay safe."

***

The next half hour was quiet compared to how things had started at the gas station. Blake and Colby continued to eat after they'd looked over Blake's foot, while Stockey let John and Allison pack up some food for the road.

Blake didn't seem to be in much pain, but I noticed Allison take another deep breath and rub at her head. "You okay?" I asked her.

"I don't feel too good," she said.

"Maybe you need to take some aspirin or something," I said. "I'll look for some."

I got up to search the small row of aisles in the gas station when there was heavy pounding on the front door. Everyone froze. My eyes immediately shot to Blake, and I noticed Colby step in my direction while keeping an arm out in front of my brother. Stockey raised his hands, silently gesturing for us to wait, and he went to the door. He let out a sigh of relief and unlocked it.

"It's all right," he said. "It's just some of my neighbors from down the road."

I nodded and let out the breath I had been holding. We could not take any more trouble.

After Stockey introduced us to everyone, we all sat back down in the middle of the store. Stockey stayed near the front, keeping an eye on the door to make sure no unwanted guests were coming our way.

Blake had finally eaten his fill and was now leaning back against one of the shelves in the snack aisle, nodding off. "Go ahead and get some rest," I told him. "You need it."

"But I need to stay awake," he mumbled, barely able to keep his eyes open. "Gotta look out for you."

"I can help with that," Colby said. "Go ahead and sleep."

Blake grinned at him at that and finally closed his eyes. I felt something in my stomach flutter but tried not to show the smile on my face. I cleared my throat and slid down against the wall to sit on the cool tile floor beside Blake. Colby sat across the aisle from me.

"So it really is an alien invasion?" we heard John ask Stockey and his neighbors.

"I was watching the news before all the power cut out," Stockey said with a nod. "They didn't know much, but the last thing they were saying was that they'd confirmed the unidentified ships weren't from Earth."

The woman sitting next to him rested her hand on her collarbone nervously. Her eyes widened. "We were watching too. And then the TV, the power, everything . . . just gone."

John gestured to the rest of our group. "We were all on a bus. It crashed around the same time the electricity died."

"I think it was an EMP blast," another man said. "Wipes out all electronics. Probably killed the car batteries too."

Everyone was quiet for a moment. "So what do we do now?" I asked.

"You're all welcome to stay here for the night," Stockey said.

John nodded. "It'll be dark out soon. At first light tomorrow morning, we'll take off."

"Let's all get some rest," Allison said.

I nodded, but I was nowhere near ready to sleep. Eventually Stockey's neighbors took off, but he volunteered to stay the night with us to make sure we were okay. The five of us stayed up talking for a few hours, while Blake snored away. I was glad. He needed all the rest he could get if his ankle was going to heal.

Eventually John and Allison settled down into a corner by themselves, Stockey went to sleep in his back office, and then it was just Colby and me.

"So your dad's in Montgomery, huh?" Colby asked.

I picked at a loose thread on my shirt. "Mm-hmm. Left about a year ago."

I could feel him watching me again. "You don't seem too happy about that."

"I'm not."

"You don't dig him too much, huh?"

"Right about now, I wish I could throw my arms around him." I looked up at Colby. "But I think I'm only feeling that way because I'm all freaked out thinking the world's gonna end. If I'm being honest . . ." I hesitated.

"Yeah, be honest."

"I've been angry with my dad ever since he left. I'm happy I didn't have to move to Montgomery with him, but I would have in a heartbeat if that meant we all could've stayed together," I said.

"Oh wait now, back up off Montgomery! There's a whole bunch of history there," Colby joked.

"Yeah, yeah, I know."

He grinned when he noticed I was trying not to smile.

I pulled my knees up and wrapped my arms around my legs. "I'm just saying it's bad enough that my mom and Blake and I had to move across the city. When my dad left, we had to downsize from a house to this tiny apartment, and I have to go to a different school," I said.

"How's that been?" Colby asked.

"Let's just say it hasn't been my favorite experience."

"So what do you want to do when you graduate?"

I looked over at him, wondering why he wanted to know. But I also didn't know what to tell him. I didn't even know if I knew the answer.

"Still trying to figure yourself out, huh?" he asked, as if reading my thoughts.

"Yeah, I guess I am. What about you?"

He shrugged. "I'm doing the same thing—trying to figure it out." He glanced down at the floor. "I'm sure you heard me talking to my grandma on the phone while we were on the bus . . ."

"Yeah, you were kind of loud and hard to ignore."

He gave a small laugh but quickly turned serious again. "So you know that I got kicked off that college visit because drugs were found in my bag—steroids. Which I've never used. Somebody gave them to me right before I headed to Hillview, but I absolutely hadn't used them. Not that my grandma believed that."

"Was she angry with you?" I asked.

"Yes, but she has a right to be. I live with her. My mom has a drug problem. If it hadn't been for my grandma—and for great teachers, coaches, and other folks in my life—I'd probably be messed up."

"So why did you have those steroids on you? Why didn't you just get rid of them?" I asked him, and then immediately wished I could take back the question. This wasn't really any of my business.

"Stupid," he mumbled. "I got cocky, thinking about trying them out—thinking that maybe with the drugs I'd be an even better player than I already am. College visits can do that to you. Five star hotel. Coaches and food all around. Endless money from an institution. And things are so competitive." He looked up at me with a serious look in his eyes. "I messed up, and now I'm out here trying to make it while aliens are attacking us. But it ain't all bad. I got to meet you at least."

I felt my heart skip a beat.

"We're gonna be okay," he said then. "You know, if the aliens don't get us. We just gotta get out of our own way. You with your anger and me with my ego."

"Yeah," I said, unable to stop the smile on my face. "Maybe we can help each other with that."

Colby nodded. He started to yawn and gave a shy smile. "Guess we'd better get some sleep too," he said.

I moved next to Blake, laying my head on the jacket he was using for a pillow. Colby curled up a few feet away from us. I smiled to myself. It's not like I was about to grab his hand or kiss him or anything, but I could tell there was definitely something between us.

CHAPTER 4

The next morning we were on the move again. Colby stuck close to Blake and me, making us both laugh by talking about normal stuff like TV and sports. With him around, it was easy to forget about the Visitors.

But even after being on the move all morning, we were still a long way from Montgomery. And walking all this way took its toll. We needed to take breaks frequently, especially with Blake's ankle still not back to one hundred percent. When we saw a rest stop sign, it was a welcome sight. We walked along the exit ramp to find a campsite with a small building for restrooms. We sat down at a picnic table and pulled out some of the food and waters we'd taken from the gas station.

John, Allison, and Blake ate quickly and headed into the building to use the restrooms afterward. Colby stayed silent even after they were gone, and I noticed he had barely eaten anything.

I nudged him to say, "Not hungry?"

He looked away.

I pressed, "Now wait, we've just been talking for hours. Why clam up on me now? What's going on?"

"It's nothing. I'm just tripping," he said.

"Tell me," I said.

"Just thinking about the future. Up until yesterday, all I could think about was getting recruited by a good college and playing football. Now I don't even know if we'll survive this alien attack. Everything I used to worry about seems kind of . . . pointless now."

"I get it. I'm second-guessing everything too. Been too angry at my folks for them splitting up, and right now I'd do anything to see them. But we've got to stay focused."

Colby looked at me and sighed. "How?"

"You're the baller. Aren't you used to figuring out how to make a comeback even when things are looking down?"

He snorted out a laugh and shook his head at me. "Yeah, I guess you're right."

I grinned at him. "I don't know that much about sports, but I know that if we want to make it we have to think we can win."

**

The weather was changing. With the darkness came the cold. We decided to stay at the campsite for the night. The building had a small hallway leading to each restroom's door. We figured we could sleep in the hallway—it was better than sleeping outside.

The five of us crammed into the small hallway together. "I'm cold, sis," Blake whispered. I motioned for him to slide closer.

Colby was on the other side of him. "Don't take your body heat away from me," he said, sliding closer too.

We didn't have a blanket, but we did have clothes from our suitcases that we draped around ourselves. I balled up a sweatshirt to rest my head on. Across from us were Allison and John.

"Let's get some rest, guys," John said. "We'll head out in the morning for our next leg." He handed Allison half a granola bar, but she groaned and turned her head away.

"My stomach is upset again," Allison mumbled. "And I have a headache. Every time it's about to rain, I get a headache."

"Don't say that," I said to her. I didn't want to add freezing fall rain to our long walk tomorrow.

"At least we have shelter for tonight," John said.

Sure enough, within a few minutes lightning was striking and thunder was roaring. John and Colby walked over to the windows to look outside. Huge drops of rain poured down.

The floor in the hallway was concrete. It wasn't comfortable, but at least it was dry. I fell asleep to the sound of the rain pounding against the roof.

CHAPTER 5

"You sure taking a bath will be okay?" I asked Allison the next day. We were walking toward a pond near the restrooms. She'd gotten up early because she wasn't feeling well and went for a walk. She found the pond and thought it would be a good chance for us to wash up before leaving.

"It looked safe to me," Allison said. "Besides, we've been walking for a few days now—I need to clean up. And it's probably a good idea to collect water where we can before we leave."

I frowned. "Yeah, but we don't know what might be in there . . ." I couldn't stop picturing snakes, leeches, all sorts of things that might give us trouble.

Allison didn't seem worried. As soon as we got to the water, I had to admit it looked incredibly inviting. Probably because I hadn't showered in days.

The thing about southern temperatures was that it could be hot one day and cold the next. Thankfully, this was a warm day even for October.

"We need to be quick about it, though," Allison said.

"You don't have to tell me." We pulled off our shoes and socks and rolled our pants up to our knees. Just bending down and splashing water on my face was refreshing. As we waded into the pond, she told me about how she and John met. It was a nice distraction from the cold water. ". . . And then I just knew he was the one," she finished.

We were quiet for a few moments, splashing the water onto our arms and faces. Then she turned to me and said, "What about you? You don't have a boyfriend, do you?"

I shook my head. I wanted to tell her I wasn't thinking about boyfriends right now, but she kept giving me a strange look.

"It's okay to like Colby," she said.

I felt heat rush into my cheeks. "Who says I do?" I shot back.

She gave me a teasing smile. "It's pretty obvious. You two seem to respond to each other. John and I even talked about it last night."

"Really," I said, not sure what to do with that piece of information.

Before I could ask her anything else, Allison threw up into the water.

When she straightened up, she sighed and wiped at the back of her mouth. "Sorry."

"That's all right," I said. "Are you okay?"

"No," she said. "I think I'm pregnant."

I stared at her. "Oh my gosh. That's . . . great."

"It's not great. Now's not the right time," Allison said. "It wasn't a good time even before this alien invasion happened, and now—I really don't know what to do."

"What does John think?"

"John doesn't know yet."

Before I could say anything else, I heard

rustling in the trees behind us. I spun around in the water, searching for any sign of a person or animal. "Did you hear that?"

But Allison was barely paying attention. "I don't hear anything, Bailey." She was looking down at the water, but I could see tears spilling over her cheeks. "I have to figure out how to tell John."

I tried to give her some space, walking along the bank of the pond while I scanned the trees for any sign of someone. But the rustling seemed to have stopped. When Allison was feeling better and we decided to head back, I still felt a little nervous. It was like somebody had been watching us.

I didn't have time to continue dwelling on it. Allison was upset about the pregnancy, and I focused on trying to make her feel better. When we got back to the restroom building, the guys were waiting for us outside. Colby and Blake were sitting together at the picnic table, and it looked like Colby was checking over Blake's ankle. I headed toward them while Allison pulled John aside.

I couldn't hear exactly what they were saying, but by the looks of their faces they were arguing. Allison began to cry again, while John just looked panicked.

Suddenly Allison took off running. John started after her but stopped after a few steps. He ran his hands through his hair. Then he looked over at us, as if we could help him.

"I'll go find her," I said.

"Bailey!" John called after me. I turned to look at him. "Tell her I'm sorry."

"Why don't you tell her that yourself?"

"Right about now, she doesn't wanna hear from me."

I rolled my eyes at him and jogged off to find Allison. I hoped she would want to hear from me. Even though I didn't know her that well, I felt her sadness and wanted to help if I could.

I didn't know which way she went, so I just went back toward the pond, figuring it was as good of a place to start as any. It wasn't until I got closer that I remembered feeling like someone had been watching us there. Before

I could give it a second thought, I heard a stifled scream.

I followed the sound, breaking into a run. When I got to the pond, I saw Allison struggling to break away from a frantic-looking older man. "Just tell us what you want from us!" he yelled at her. "Tell us why you came here!"

"I don't know what you're talking about!" cried Allison.

"You think you can fool me by disguising yourself as a human? I know you're an alien! I know the Visitors are walking among us."

"I'm not an alien," Allison protested. "I swear!"

"You don't wanna make me angry," he growled. "You're not going to outsmart me. Tell me what your plan is, or I'll make you regret you ever came to Earth!"

CHAPTER 6

"Hey—leave her alone!" I shouted.

My voice echoed through the trees, making the attacker pause. He turned around to look in the direction of my voice. I bent down to pick up the nearest heavy stick. "I said leave her alone!"

When he saw me waving the stick at him, he let go of Allison and dashed away. I lowered the stick and ran up to Allison, asking if she was okay.

"There y'all are," John said, rushing over to Allison. Colby was right behind him. "What happened? I heard screaming."

"We're okay," Allison said. "Some guy thought I was an alien. He was completely freaking out. I'm not sure what he would've done if Bailey hadn't chased him off."

John hugged her tightly. "It's my fault. I'm sorry I upset you so much," he said to her. "You wouldn't have run off alone like that if hadn't freaked out at you. And you, Bailey," he looked over at me. "I let you go get her. It should've been me."

"I think this guy's been following us, though," I said. "When we were cleaning up earlier, I felt like somebody was watching us. If I would've gone with my first instinct, maybe I would've told you guys. Maybe I would've been more on the lookout . . ."

Allison reached over to squeeze my hand. "This wasn't your fault. You're the whole reason I didn't get hurt!"

I let out a shaky breath and finally dropped the stick I'd been holding. I couldn't be strong anymore. I couldn't act like I had it all together. I couldn't pretend everything was fine. What if the guy came back or we ran into others like him? I felt more afraid of that than of any actual aliens.

"Let's just get out of here," I said, my throat tight.

Colby caught up to me as I walked back to the campsite. "I ain't even gonna ask if you're okay because I can tell you're not," he said quietly. "But you're not alone, all right? If we all stick together, this kind of thing won't happen again."

Hearing him say that, I felt some of my strength being restored.

***

We were walking up a steep hill when we heard someone hollering for help. We picked up our speed and when we reached the top, we noticed a bridge at the bottom of the other side of the hill. A man was standing down there, near where an SUV was hanging over the edge of the bridge, just about to tip over and fall into the river.

"Please help me!" the man cried when he saw us. "My family's inside."

We jogged down to get to them. A woman was sitting in the front seat and a girl around my age was in the back. They looked terrified.

"Stay calm," John said to the man. "I've got some rope. We can use that to pull them up."

"That car weighs a lot more than we do," Colby pointed out. "We'll need to anchor the rope to something sturdy."

I looked around. The road on either side of the bridge was narrow, but on the other side was a line of tall oak trees. "How about one of those trees?" I suggested.

It didn't take long for us to secure one end of the rope to a tree and the other end to the SUV. Then we each lined up to grab a section of the rope. Blake's ankle was still bothering him, so I made him sit off to the side.

With each of us pulling on the rope, we quickly made progress. Colby stood at the end as the anchor. He was tugging the hardest, and he groaned with each flex of his arms. The SUV's front wheels began to roll backward, and soon the whole vehicle was securely back on the bridge.

"Oh, thank you!" the man said. He rushed over to get to the SUV while the rest of us took some deep breaths.

Colby walked out of his stance, shaking his hands.

Then I heard a strange cracking sound. My first thought was that it was another attack from the Visitors, but when I turned toward the sound it was coming from, I realized it was something else.

The tree we'd tied the rope to must have been dead in the center. The weight from the car and us pulling had caused it to crack.

And the tree was tipping over right in Colby's direction.

CHAPTER 7

"Colby!" I shouted.

Instincts kicked in when I saw the tree falling toward him. I sprinted toward him, tackling him to the ground a few feet away. We rolled as we hit the ground, and the tree just missed us.

"Bailey!" Blake shouted. I could hear him, Allison, and John rushing over to us, but I was still trying to get my bearings.

I had fallen on top of Colby, and when I moved to push myself up I got caught in his dark eyes. He was staring back at me. His arms had wrapped around me. It felt like we were in a bubble. Sounds were rushing all around me—I could hear the others trying to ask us if we were okay.

I'd never felt this way with a boy before. Feeling a little freaked out, I got up and dashed back to the car. I told myself it was because I wanted to make sure the others were okay, but I mostly just wanted to get some space from Colby. I didn't know what to think of what I was feeling. In its own way, it was more surprising than anything else that had happened to me in the last few days.

Allison reached for me as I came over. "Are you all right?" she asked.

I nodded, breathless.

She seemed to notice that I needed some space, so she led John over to check on the family. Blake hovered around me with wide eyes, clearly worried but not sure what he could do. I couldn't say anything to him yet. I didn't even know what I could do right now.

Colby slowly got up from the ground and came over to us.

"Thank you," he said. "I didn't even notice the tree. It would've landed right on me if you hadn't reacted so fast."

Blake grinned up at Colby as if he was his personal hero. "You saved me and my sister on the bus," he said. "Now she saved you. So we're even."

Colby smirked at him. "I don't know. I still feel like I owe a big debt to her."

Blake didn't seem to notice the tension between Colby and me. But the way Colby was staring at me made my heart kick into a rapid pace. I heard Allison call for Blake to come over, but it sounded much farther away than it should have been. I barely noticed Blake wander away from us.

"Like my brother said, you've already done the same. You owe me nothing," I said quietly. Colby just kept staring down at me.

Is he going to kiss me? I couldn't help but wonder. That thought made my stomach twist into knots. I still wasn't sure how to react if he did make a move.

I cleared my throat and took a step back. "We should make sure the others are okay," I said, dropping my eyes. I turned to follow after Blake.

I could feel Colby's disappointment, but I didn't know what else to do. Besides, I needed to focus on getting my brother home, and Colby was starting to be a distraction I did *not* need.

Allison must have noticed the entire exchange. As I joined the others, she gave me a look and I shook my head to say I didn't want to talk about it right now.

Thankfully, we had something else to keep everyone's attention.

"Thank you all for your help," the dad said after his family had climbed out of the SUV. "My name is Dennis and this is my wife Greta. Our daughter over there is Daphne."

We each introduced ourselves. I couldn't help but notice that Daphne stared up at Colby the entire time.

"How did you guys manage to get your SUV over the edge of the bridge anyway?" John asked.

"When the news first came out about the alien lights," Dennis explained, "we heard about a nearby emergency shelter the Army was setting up. We packed up everything we could and headed out immediately. We were making good time until that blast yesterday morning."

"People think it was an EMP," Allison said.

Greta nodded. "We heard the same thing."

"We had too much with us to carry on foot and we didn't want to leave the SUV in case there was a chance of getting it working again eventually, so we've been trying to push the SUV along. We made it to the top of the hill, and I thought it would be easy for us to put it in neutral and let the girls ride inside on the way down."

He shook his head. "What a stupid mistake. I'm so grateful you folks came along when you did."

"Yeah, that was amazing," Daphne said, stepping closer to Colby. I couldn't help but grit my teeth.

"You mentioned a shelter," Allison said. "Where is it?"

"It's at the community college in Merrimont," Dennis explained.

Merrimont was only a few miles north of Montgomery. If it was going to get me closer to my dad, I was for it. I wanted to see my dad again, hug him, and let him know how much I missed him. How sorry I was for being angry with him. And how I was thankful for him, even when I'd been distant.

So we all got behind Dennis and Greta's SUV and took turns helping to push it up the gravel road. Even Blake wanted to help push, but I told him it would put too much strain on his ankle.

For a while we talked about the big elephant in the sky—the alien invasion. But no one had real answers. Just more of the same questions: where are they, and what do they want?

Finally Dennis said, "You know, I was so afraid of what this attack might mean, but today, after my family was dangling off a bridge and strangers coming in to help us, I'm not worried anymore. None of us knows what the future holds. But we can live each day with gratitude."

I nodded at what Dennis said but then frowned when I noticed Daphne was walking next to Colby again.

"Who cares about aliens when you got big, strong guys around to make sure you're okay?" Daphne said, feeling on Colby's shoulder. "Oh, you got muscles. You're strong. You play football or something?"

I just rolled my eyes. Did she have to be so obvious?

"I used to, yeah, but it's not just guys who can be the heroes. She saved me earlier." Colby pointed at me.

Daphne gave me a fake smile. "Yeah, that's great that your sister was there."

Really? I thought to myself.

Colby snorted. "Uh, she's not my sister."

Daphne gave an innocent shrug, but I saw right through it.

"Oh, well I just assumed she was," she said. "I mean, why else would she wanna save you like that? You only get that kind of courage when it's someone you care about. You know, like a family member."

Colby looked over at me with a smirk. "Oh, yeah? Bailey, do you think of me like a brother?"

I didn't know how to respond. With all that was going on in the world, I couldn't believe I was on front street about my feelings.

I rolled my eyes at Daphne again and picked up my pace. Every step I took away from Colby bothered me on the inside, but I wasn't ready to let him know I liked him.

CHAPTER 8

"Wait up, Bailey. Let me talk to you," Colby said, catching me off guard.

I kept walking and didn't say anything.

He sped up to catch up to me. "You're mad."

"How could you tell?" I answered sarcastically.

"Oh, so it's gonna be like that?"

"How's it supposed to be, Colby? This girl is all over you and you're not doing anything to discourage it."

"Why do you even care?" he asked with a wide grin. He reached over and nudged my arm.

I stumbled over a way to answer him, and that only made him grin even more.

"Look, I'm not trying to get you to admit anything here. I don't even know what I'm feeling either, but it's clear something's going on between us. I mean, you saved my life!"

"I would've done that for anybody."

"Yeah, maybe you would've. But you did it for me, and it matters. I'm always saving someone else. My grandma. Working a couple extra hours to bring more money into the house for her. Or my teammates. Before I joined the team, they had no chance at the state title. I started playing when I was a freshman, and now we're on the radar. Ever since then, everyone at my school has expected me to lead the team to State every year."

I gave him a blank look. If he wanted to impress someone with his football stats, he should be talking to Blake, not me. "So what are you saying?" I asked.

"I don't know. You know I'm not perfect. I got kicked off my recruiting visit. Ever since all this stuff happened with the Visitors, I've been rethinking what I'm doing with my life. And when I needed help, you were there for me."

"And you've been there for me too,"
I admitted.

"So what do we do with all of this?"
Colby asked.

I had no idea, but I did know that if the
Visitors continued their attack on Earth, at least
I had a chance to feel something I'd never felt
with a boy before—a deep flutter in my heart.

But I still didn't know how to say that
to him.

He took my hand. "Maybe . . . whatever
this is, we don't have to give a name to it.
Could be like the aliens, you know?"

I nodded. "Yeah, we know they're out
there. Even though we can't see them . . ."

Colby squeezed my hand and said,
"They're here."

***

I didn't know how many people lived in
Alabama, but there was a whole bunch at the
shelter on the Merrimont campus. A lot of
those people were Army personnel. There
were working Army trucks too—Dennis

figured they must've been safe in some reinforced bunker when the EMP knocked out everything else.

We were told to check in at one of the college's main office buildings. As our group walked in, I heard some officers talking about using the Army trucks to send messages through other shelters within a fifty mile radius.

When the adults turned our way, their conversation stopped and they were all business. As they handed us some forms to fill out, I asked, "Do we have any answers as to what's going on with the Visitors?" If the Army didn't know, the rest of us had no hope of figuring anything out.

One of the officers said, "Bits of information are coming in. The alien attack is confirmed to have been an EMP blast, and there are some reports of smaller alien vessels coming from the motherships. But no confirmed sightings of the aliens themselves. Rescue and humanitarian organizations continue to get supplies from underground storage sites that were unaffected by the EMP, and they're working on setting up more shelters. Meanwhile we're assigning people here to rooms and providing meals. Electricity is still out, but plumbing is mostly working."

"My brother and I are trying to get to Montgomery," I told her. "Our dad is there."

She wrote the names *Bailey Clarke* and *Blake Clarke* on their list of unaccompanied minors. Then she handed us several pieces of blank paper. "We're asking all unaccompanied minors and other people who've been separated from loved ones to write down your names and any information that could help us locate your families. It'll help to write something that will confirm your identity for your parents. With all the chaos right now, they might not be sure who to trust."

I couldn't imagine why someone would contact my parents pretending to be me. But then I remembered hearing about trolls setting up fake social media accounts for victims of disasters. Sometimes they did it to raise money, sometimes they just wanted to mess with people. Even though we didn't have internet access, some people might be doing the same thing with letters.

I thanked the Army officer and took my writing materials over to a small table in the corner of the room. Colby got his own pen and paper and joined me there.

An officer led Dennis and Greta's family away to bring them to their room. While Allison and John waited for us, we got to work.

I wrote two letters—one to my dad and one to my mom. At the top, I wrote their addresses and job titles. Then I got to the hard part.

I hope this letter finds you. It's your Bailey, and I'm with Blake. We're at the community college in Merrimont. The Army told us to write something so that you would know it's your real children. Well, how about this: I've been a jerk, not really accepting that you guys are separated. Just upset for a year that I had to uproot my world. How selfish of me. Please forgive me for being angry.

Blake and I have had some bumps and bruises, but we are okay. When I see you, I can only imagine the reunion. Love you so much.

Yours,

Bailey

It was a relief to finally be real with my parents, even if it was just by letter. Truth was, I didn't know if I'd see them again. But I had to hold on to hope that we would be reunited.

Once we'd finished the paperwork, the officer who'd answered my questions asked us to follow her. She brought us to a hall lined with offices. "We're a little tight on space right now," the officer explained. "The campus dorms have all filled up, so we're housing people in other buildings too." As we walked down the hallway, I noticed that every room was packed with families. Sleeping bags and packs covered the floors.

The officer stopped at one of the empty rooms. "You five can stay in here."

We filed in, taking in the space. There was a desk with a rolling chair, a wall of shelves and cabinets, and one overstuffed armchair. No windows, so the officer handed us a single candle and a small matchbook. "We're, ah, also a little light on resources," she said with a tight smile.

"We'll make do," Allison said, though I saw her place a protective hand on her stomach.

"The dining hall is serving dinner until seven tonight," the officer added. "Feel free to head over there once you've gotten settled. Breakfast is from eight to nine in the morning."

I wished my phone still worked just so that I could set an alarm. Luckily John had an old-fashioned watch that was still ticking away. He promised to keep track of time so we wouldn't miss dinner.

We gave Blake the armchair so he could try to keep his leg elevated. The rest of us took spots on the floor. Allison and John made a little nest behind the desk for some privacy. That left Colby and me sleeping on the floor in the front of the small office space. We would be sleeping directly next to each other. I tried not to think about it.

After setting up, we grubbed at the campus dining hall. I made sure Blake got plenty to eat. He hadn't complained about his foot all day, but now that he didn't have to walk on it as much, his mood definitely improved. In fact, everyone seemed to be in better spirits. John was making sure Allison was comfortable, rubbing gently on her belly, and even talking to it. She just chuckled, and I loved that. It felt like another sign that life as we knew it wasn't gone completely.

CHAPTER 9

The next morning, I woke up to my brother's moans. I rolled over and saw him clutching at his foot. When I tried to look at it, he shouted louder and scrunched up his face.

"It hurts, bad," he groaned.

"What's going on?" John asked sleepily.

"We need help—something is wrong with Blake!" I shouted.

Colby got up and sprinted out into the hall.

Blake lifted the leg of his sweatpants to reveal that his ankle was swollen again and looking a sickly color. I could hear footsteps pounding in the hallway and Colby's voice.

"You're gonna be fine," I said to Blake, trying to use a soothing voice. "Help is coming. You hang in there. You've already made it this far."

Colby led two Army medics into the room. Allison pulled me back so they could look at Blake. His face was scrunched up with pain, and as soon as one of the medics shifted his ankle, Blake screamed. Hearing that sound, I felt like I was going to pass out.

Colby grabbed my hand and dragged me into the hallway.

I couldn't help myself this time—I broke down into tears. Colby wrapped his arms around me and let me cry against his chest. I couldn't handle it if something happened to my brother.

Allison's voice drifted over to us. I could hear her speaking calmly to Blake, telling him everything would be all right. I hoped she was holding his hand when I couldn't be there to do it.

After a minute or so, the screaming stopped and Blake seemed to be calming down. I turned in Colby's arms to see the medics stepping out of the room.

One of them approached me. "They said you're his sister?"

I nodded, wiping the tears from my cheeks. I stepped away from Colby. "How is he?" I asked.

"He's gonna be just fine. It's difficult to tell without an x-ray, but we think it's a sprain. He must have agitated it in his sleep—all that walking wasn't good for it either. We've fitted him with a brace and gave him some ibuprofen. He can come see us every few hours for another dose."

"Okay," I said. That didn't seem too bad. I could handle that.

"Keep him off his feet for the next day or so," the medic added.

"Thank you so much."

As they walked away, I smiled at Colby. He wiped a stray tear from my cheek. I laughed, embarrassed.

"See?" he said. "Everything's gonna be okay."

But apparently he'd spoken too soon. Down at the far end of the hall, someone screamed out, "The faucet is putting out brown water!"

So not only did we have no power, but now we could add plumbing problems to the list. What was next? I certainly didn't want to know the answer.

***

Over the next several days, people kept showing up at the campus. Most were looking for food and shelter just like us. But plenty were also looking for family members. I saw parents and grandparents clutching handwritten letters just like the ones I'd sent to my mom and dad. And I saw little kids, teens, even some grown people tearfully embrace the new arrivals.

Once these families were reunited, they didn't leave the shelter. Instead they hunkered down. The office building where we spent most of our time had gotten even more crowded, with people and their belongings clogging up the hallways and common areas. The bathrooms were a nightmare. And at meals I noticed that the dining hall filled up, and the officers in charge started distributing smaller portions of food. But none of that was my main concern.

By the end of the week I was pretty sure Colby, Blake, and I were the only kids who didn't have their families with them.

I was beginning to wonder if our parents would ever find us. But I didn't want to worry the others, especially Blake.

Colby, however, seemed to notice my darkening mood. He took me aside one morning after we'd finished eating. "Hey," he said. "I want to talk to you about something."

"Okay."

"And I need you to have an open mind."

I arched an eyebrow at him. "Okay . . ."

"I'm serious, Bailey. We've been here for almost two weeks now and neither of us have heard anything from our families." He lowered his voice and checked over his shoulders. "Camp conditions are getting real bad—we're gonna run out of food soon, and they bring in new people every day. We need to flip things."

I squinted up at him. I didn't know where he was going with this, but I was beginning to feel worried about it.

He looked back at me, resting his hands on my shoulders. "There's a group of folks who're gonna try to steal one of the Army trucks and make it to Montgomery tomorrow."

"Wait a minute," I hissed. "What are you talking about? You've been telling me you want to start living your life the right way. How does stealing an Army vehicle fit into that plan?"

"It ain't even like the surveillance cameras and stuff are working, Bailey. I'm not gonna get caught."

He'd completely missed my point, so I tried a different angle. "I know things are bad here," I said. "But we just sent out those letters to our folks. What if we leave and they finally get here?"

"What if they're waiting for you in Montgomery right now?" he shot back. "We don't even know if those letters got to them. Look, I still have my license on me. I can drive. You and Blake can—"

"No," I cut him off, shrugging his hands off my shoulders. "I don't want to take that chance. And my brother and I are going nowhere with you in some stolen vehicle."

He crossed his arms and looked away. "Suit yourself, then."

"Yeah, suit *yourself*, then."

Before he could say anything else, I walked away. I hated being at odds with him, but I had to stand my ground. I didn't want to be a part of this—and there was no way I was going to let Blake.

I went back to the living quarters. There was a small reception area in one of the office spaces that everyone had turned into a community space. The rest of our group plus a few others were sitting in the cluster of couches and armchairs. Everyone seemed so somber.

"What if this is the end?" Greta was asking. "What if the lights and power never come back on? How could we survive?"

"What if the Visitors come down here and attack us?" asked a guy.

"Who knows what they might do," an older

woman pitched in. "They might even take some of us to their world."

Allison was tearing up. "I get what I've always wanted, and my baby might not even have a chance."

"I just wanted to play football," Blake said. "I get to finally meet a five-star player who can give me some pointers, and I might not even get to use what he told me."

"I just got a promotion at work," Greta said. "Now, I'll probably never get to see that first paycheck."

Tired of the negative vibes, I sat up straight in my seat. "Okay, okay, we gotta stay positive. I know it's important to be realistic, but we don't even know what's really going on. So hanging onto hope will keep us moving. We don't know what's going to happen with the Visitors yet."

I turned to Allison and John. "Your baby is going to be amazing. You're going to give it a good life."

"And Blake." I looked over at my little brother, who was watching me with wide eyes.

"Maybe you won't get to grow up and become a five-star athlete—maybe you will. Either way, you'll still be able to use those skills."

Blake gave a small laugh then. "Yeah, maybe someday I'll get to tackle some alien butt."

The rest of the group laughed at that, and I could tell spirits were lifting. Maybe our lives wouldn't turn out the way we'd all imagined for ourselves, but we were still holding on. We'd get through this.

CHAPTER 10

The next morning when we showed up at the dining hall for breakfast, an Army officer told us there wouldn't be a morning meal today. "We're cutting back until we can top up our food supply," he explained.

"How long is that going to take?" I asked, but he didn't have an answer.

"What are we gonna eat?" Blake asked me. I didn't know how to answer him.

I looked at him and said, "Come on, let's go back to our room. There's still some food in our suitcase."

Over the past week resources had become increasingly scarce. We'd run out of soap. The rations of bottled water were running low. And since things were tight, the people were very irritable. Fights were breaking out, and the hopefulness I'd been trying so hard to hold onto a few days ago already seemed like a distant memory.

Back in our room, I opened up a pack of peanut butter crackers for Blake and me to split for breakfast, just like we'd been doing for the past few days now. I was sick of peanut butter crackers. But it was better than the cans of sardines sitting in my backpack.

"Here," I said, handing another pack of crackers to Blake. "Go give these to Colby."

He'd been avoiding me for the past week, but I knew he hadn't been eating much. Even though I was still annoyed with him, I couldn't help but worry about him.

Blake wandered down the hall in search of Colby. Allison and John were sitting with me, and I watched as John gave up his breakfast for the third morning in a row so Allison could have more to eat. He took some sips of a sports drink, insisting that he wasn't really that hungry anyway. Allison sniffled to herself as she scarfed down the protein bar. I could tell she didn't want to take away John's share, but she also knew she had to keep herself as well fed as possible for their baby.

My stomach twisted. *How long can we last like this?* I wondered.

Blake came back to me with the packet of crackers in his hand. "We'll have to give it to him another time. He just jetted out. Did he tell you about his plan?"

I frowned and brought him out into the hall so Allison and John wouldn't hear us. "Did he tell *you* about his plan?" I whispered.

"Uh—yeah. He's gonna get a truck."

Huffing in frustration, I nodded. "*Steal* a truck. He didn't ask you to go with him or anything, did he?"

"No, no. I mean, I'm only in eighth grade. I don't even have a license. But I said I'd be the lookout person."

I glared at him. "Don't even talk stupid."

"I'm just playing. But he said he's coming back, and if he gets a car, we need to be ready."

I put my hand on my hip and rolled my

eyes at Blake. He put his hands up innocently but said, "For real, for real. If he comes back with a car, I'm tossing in. Look around here. People don't even have anything to eat. And we gotta get to Dad."

I sighed, knowing that underneath Blake's worshipping of Colby, he was really trying to find a way to help. "We *will* see Dad soon, but this isn't the way to make that happen. Even if I felt okay about using a stolen Army truck as a getaway vehicle, I don't think it's a good idea for us to leave Merrimont. Dad or Momma might be trying to get here right now."

Blake nodded. "So when Colby's gone, it's just gonna be you and me."

I turned to him with a big smile, nudged him in the arm, and said, "Not bad company."

Blake laughed, but I knew he was worried about the same things that were keeping me up at night: Would we see our folks again? What was going to happen with the Visitors? How long would we be able to stay here before the Army ran out of resources?

***

Wasn't long at all before Colby walked back into the room. Blake ran straight up to him as if nothing was wrong with his ankle. They said a few words. I pretended to be focused on the book in my hands, but I couldn't help myself from peeking over at them every few seconds.

Out of the corner of my eye, I watched as Colby dropped his bag back into his sleeping space. Then Blake went over to our suitcase, discreetly got the crackers back out, and handed them to Colby. I smiled inwardly, realizing Colby must have changed his mind.

Colby didn't look my way. Probably didn't want me to say "I told you so." Not that I would've done that.

Later in the evening, though, Colby did come over to me. "Can we talk?"

"What's going on?" I asked.

"So I had planned on going with that group of guys to get a truck, but at the last minute I decided not to." He rubbed a hand on the back of his head. "I just heard they got caught. Didn't even make it off the campus."

I sighed. "That doesn't surprise me. I'm just glad you backed out before it was too late."

"Me too."

He was still looking at me, so I asked, "Do you have something else to say?"

"I just want to apologize for being a jerk, that's all."

I guess I'd been secretly hoping for a little more than that. My heart dropped, but I tried not to show my disappointment. "That's all? Oh, okay. Well, I accept your apology."

Before I could turn around, he gently touched my arm. "I also want to thank you for talking some sense into me when I wanted to take the quick way out."

"You were mad at me for it," I said.

"Yeah, I was," he admitted. "Looking back at it all, I know you only had my best interest in mind. And me being angry really had nothing to do with you. I knew what was the right thing to do, but I was battling with it. Went out with those guys and was ready to steal a car because that's what I thought was best, and look what happened. Almost got myself into trouble again."

I gave him a slight smile. "I get it. I haven't been perfect either, but I do wanna get better."

"Oh yeah?"

I paused and chose my words carefully. "I want to get better about my pride—opening up and letting people know how I feel about them."

"Maybe we can help each other," he said, smiling.

"I'd like that."

"Well, you're admitting that?" he teased. "It's a start."

I laughed, and he reached out to hug me. Boy, did the embrace feel good.

CHAPTER 11

That night was probably the first time in my whole life that I didn't have a meal at dinner time. I didn't know how I was going to sleep on an empty stomach.

I couldn't help thinking about my parents. Where were they? Had they gotten my letters? If they hadn't, I knew my mom had to be worried out of her mind. My dad would be turning over every stone in search of us. Meaning if we got to Montgomery, he might not even be there. He might already be headed back to Atlanta, trying to find us. I felt so frustrated. I was used to the days of texting and IM and email, where I heard back from my parents almost instantly.

Now, I had no idea where they were or if they even knew we were okay.

I could only clasp my hands together, release my fears, and have faith that everything was going to be okay—even though I was trying to suppress my feelings of not really believing everything was going to be okay. With each passing day, things weren't getting better. They were getting worse.

I was awakened by Allison the next morning. "You guys gotta go. Come on."

"Where are we going?" I asked, rubbing at my eyes.

"There's a new plan," she said. "And it's going to get you closer to your family. Come see this."

Colby and Blake were already outside waiting for us. "What's going on?" I asked.

Blake excitedly pointed at a huge green Army truck with the engine running. "It's a transport!" he told me. "They're moving us to another shelter—in Montgomery!"

I noticed the group waiting by the truck with their packed belongings were all kids.

And there was a cardboard sign hanging from the back of the truck that read:

EIGHTEEN AND UNDER ONLY

Colby grabbed my hand. "I need to talk to you, please."

I noticed he had his belongings with him. "You're leaving?" I asked in disbelief.

"We should all be leaving. You, me, and Blake. They're taking kids whose families haven't found them yet to this other shelter just for minors. It's in Montgomery, like Blake just said. Which means—"

I cut him off. "I'm not leaving. Blake and I are staying put."

"Why? We should stay together."

I jerked my hand away from his. "Then don't leave. I sent those messages to my parents—you sent a letter to your grandma. They're coming here for us. They could be on the way to Merrimont right now. What's the use of getting all the way to Montgomery if it turns out our folks aren't there?"

I could tell Colby was losing his patience. "If they were coming to Merrimont, don't you think they would have already been here by now?"

"Not if they have to walk!"

"Other families had to walk from even farther away, and they've already gotten their kids. We need to go *look* for our folks. Maybe they're stuck in Montgomery. Maybe they never even got our letters!"

"I know that's a possibility," I said quietly, looking down at my feet. "But . . . something is telling me we should stay put. At least for a little longer."

Colby sighed. "Your choice." He took me gently by the arm and pulled me to a quiet place around the corner. "But Bailey, look, before we make any other decisions, I just have to tell you . . . I think you're beautiful."

My heart raced at his words. I hadn't had a decent shower in weeks. I hadn't even brushed my teeth yet this morning. And here he was, calling me beautiful.

"You're smart," he continued. "And you're tough. You push me to want to be better."

I had no clue where he was going with

this, but I couldn't move a muscle. When he leaned in and put his lips to mine, I felt like I was floating. Like we were floating, suspended through time. Like this was the best moment of my life. And then he abruptly backed away.

"I'm sorry," he said.

"What for?" My stomach dropped at the thought that maybe I'd done something wrong. I'd never kissed a boy before. "Did I . . ."

"No, no, it's not that," he said, giving me a genuine smile. "You did fine."

I touched my lips, wanting this feeling to never end.

"Please," he tried again. "Come with me. When we get to this new shelter you can write to your parents again. Or we can look for them on our own."

And suddenly the feeling was gone. Colby was sweet, but it bothered me that he wouldn't respect my decision. "I told you I can't do that," I responded softly. I couldn't explain what I was feeling. It wasn't just hurt. It wasn't just anger or sadness. Maybe it was a little bit of all of it rolled up into one, and I needed to be away from him. He just needed to go.

Colby reached for me again.

"Stay strong, Bailey. Take care—"

"No, just stop, Colby. Just go. I don't need you kissing me and acting like you care. I'm done with your mixed messages."

CHAPTER 12

I watched Colby line up with the other kids and teenagers to board the transport truck. I didn't want to be the girl watching him leave, so I walked around the corner to get some air. I leaned back against the brick of the building and wiped the tears as they sprung from my eyes.

Even though Colby and I didn't exactly see eye to eye, I could admit to myself now that I cared about him. I wasn't expecting him leaving to hurt this much. After a few minutes, Blake found me. His eyes were watery, and I realized I wasn't the only one breaking down because of this. I hugged him tight.

"We're gonna figure this out."

"I don't think so anymore," he said. "We should go with Colby. Please, Bailey. We can protect each other. Please."

"But Momma and Dad will be coming to find us here . . ." I said.

I didn't know what to do. What if we left and our parents came here? But what if we stayed, while our parents were busy looking for us in Atlanta and Montgomery?

"What if the letters never got to them?" Blake mumbled. "What if Momma and Dad never find us?"

"I wouldn't worry about that," we heard a familiar voice say.

Shocked, we pulled away from each other to see our dad grinning at us. You wouldn't even be able to tell Blake had hurt his ankle by the way he ran over to our dad.

I could see one of the Army officers watching us, looking to confirm that we knew this man. I just put my hand over my mouth and nodded. He gave me a thumbs-up and moved back to the truck. I dashed to my dad then too.

"Daddy!" He stepped away from Blake and opened his arms wide as I rushed over to him. I burst into tears again. "I'm so sorry, Dad. I know I've been distant and mad. After everything that's happened, I've just wanted to be able to tell you how much I love you."

"I know, honey," he said as he pulled out one of my letters. "When your mother and I got your messages—"

"Wait, Momma?"

He nodded. "She's talking with one of the officers out front to get you signed out."

Even before he finished talking, our mom walked over to us. Blake took off running again. He tackled her, and I was right behind him. "I can't believe you're both here!" I choked out.

"Your dad and I ran into each other at the front entrance," my mom explained as she hugged Blake and me. "What are the chances of that?"

Suddenly I froze. Not because I wasn't excited to see my mom, but because there was someone familiar standing right behind her.

Colby walked up to me and said, "Looks like those letters worked after all."

"Guess so," I said as my heart fluttered. "I thought you were going to the other shelter."

"I am, but the truck had to make a last-minute stop. And I realized I couldn't go without knowing you and Blake were okay." Colby gently brushed my cheek. Our eyes locked. My dad coughed. I came back to reality with a hot flush in my cheeks. We quickly stepped away from each other.

Allison and John walked over to us. They were grinning at us, plainly seeing that Blake and I had finally been reunited with our parents. I introduced everyone.

As our parents thanked Allison and John for watching out for us, I turned to Colby. "I guess this means we'll be going back to Atlanta. I don't know if I'll see you again."

"Actually," my mom said, "with all that's going on, your dad and I have agreed we should all be together for the time being. We're going back to Montgomery until things have settled down."

"We're heading in that direction too," Allison said. She looked at Colby. "And, Colby, since we're the ones who brought you here, we should be able to sign you out to leave with us." She winked at me. "If you'd like to tag along with everyone to Montgomery . . ."

Colby grinned. "That would be great."

Blake cheered, causing the adults to laugh. I couldn't help but laugh with them. I even felt brave enough to grab Colby's hand in front of my parents.

I didn't know what tomorrow would bring. We still hadn't heard anything about the Visitors, and no one had any idea if we'd ever get the electricity back. Ever since the attack, I'd been trying to get home, but I now knew that as long as I was with those I cared about, I was already home.

ATTACK ON EARTH

WHEN ALIENS INVADE, ALL YOU CAN DO IS SURVIVE

DESERTED

THE FALLOUT

THE FIELD TRIP

GETTING HOME

LOCKDOWN

TAKE SHELTER

CHECK OUT ALL THE TITLES IN THE
ATTACK ON EARTH SERIES

LEVEL UP

WHAT WOULD YOU DO IF YOU WOKE UP IN A VIDEO GAME?

ALIEN INVASION
ISRAEL KEATS

LABYRINTH
ISRAEL KEATS

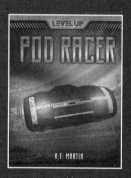

POD RACER
R.T. MARTIN

REALM OF MYSTICS
RAELYN DRAKE

SAFE ZONE
R.T. MARTIN

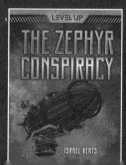

THE ZEPHYR CONSPIRACY
ISRAEL KEATS

ABOUT THE AUTHOR

Stephanie Perry Moore is truly from the south. She was born in South Carolina, raised in Virginia, educated in Alabama, and now lives in Georgia. She is the author of many YA series, including the Sharp Sisters series, the Swoop List series, the Lockwood Lions series, the Grovehill Giants series, the Payton Skky series, the Laurel Shadrach series, the Perry Skky Jr. series, the Beta Gamma Pi series, and the Yasmin Peace series. She and her husband, Derrick Moore, have three children: Dustyn, Sydni, and Sheldyn.